My Mom Is Different

by Deborah Sessions

Illustrations by Susan Chalkley

The Sidran Press

Grateful acknowledgement is made to Random House, Inc. for permission to reprint from *Horton Hears a Who* by Dr. Seuss. TM and copyright 1954 by The 1984 Geisel Trust.

International Standard Book Number: 0-9629164-3-9
Library of Congress Card Catalogue Number: 93-46388
Printed in the United States of America

Sessions, Deborah.
My mom is different / by Deborah Sessions ; illustrations by Susan Chalkley.
p. cm.
ISBN 0-9629164-3-9 : $8.95
1. Multiple personality—Juvenile literature. 2. Children of the mentally ill—Juvenile literature. [1. Multiple personality. 2. Mentally ill. 3. Mother and child.] I. Chalkley, Susan, ill.
II. Title.
RC569.5.M8S47 1994
616.85'236—dc20 93-46388
CIP AC

This book is dedicated to my husband, Gene,

&

my sons,

Benjamin, Peter, and Nathaniel

I love my mom, but my mom is different from my friends' moms. She has MPD. That is Multiple Personality Disorder. She does strange things sometimes. She has been in the hospital. But lots of times she is just like herself, my regular mom.

I know she loves me very much because she is always telling me that no matter what she does or says I will always be special to her.

She has MPD because people did very bad and scary things to her when she was a little girl. She was afraid she would get into trouble if she said anything to anyone, so she kept all the bad things a secret and never told anyone.

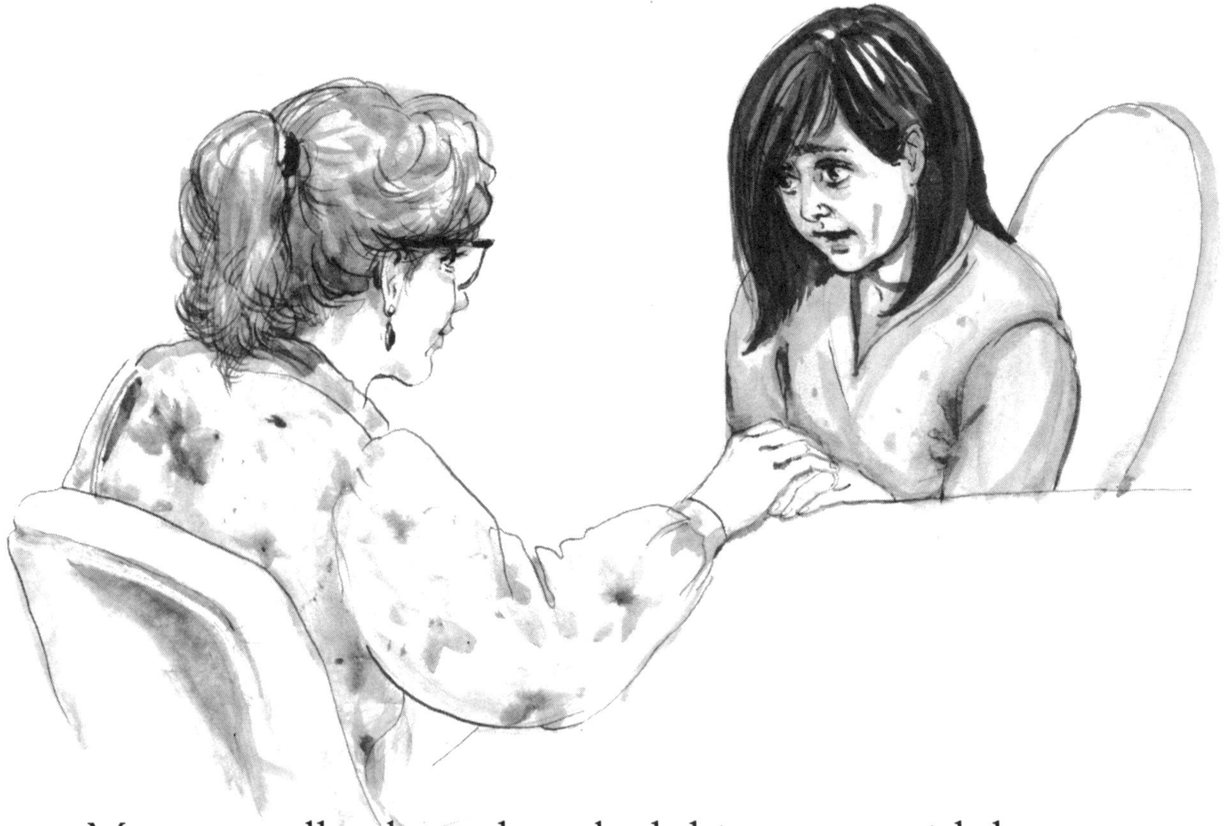

My mom talks about those bad things now with her therapist. A therapist is a person who knows how to listen carefully and help people learn to solve their problems. A therapist helps people talk about their secrets so they need not be afraid anymore.

Sometimes I feel scared of my mom's therapist. I feel like I don't know her very well. I wonder what she does with my mom when she goes to the office. I wonder if they talk about me. My mom says they only talk about her memories.

My mom says her therapist is a good person and is very important to her. She is my mom's partner and guide who helps my mom when her memories are frightening.

Talking with her therapist about the past is hard for my mom and lots of times she gets upset. It brings back bad memories about what happened to her as a child. But she says talking is good for her, even if it makes her cry. That is the only way the bad feelings will go away and she can be happier.

Sometimes, when the talking is too hard, my mom gets very sad and cries all the time. Other times she won't talk to us or she does strange things. She has even done things to hurt herself.

Then she has to go to the hospital for a while. Sometimes it is for a long time but other times it is not very long. But I hate it. I get mad at her for being in the hospital, and for being different from other moms who stay at home.

I don't like to visit the hospital too much. It makes me sad to see my mom there. When she cries, I don't know what to do. She tells me it helps her when I come to visit her there, so I go.

Mom asks me to tell her how I feel even if it makes her cry. She wants me to be free to tell whatever I feel and to know that it is okay. She says she could never tell about her feelings when she was a little girl.

When I cry and say, "I'm mad at you. I want you to come home. I don't want you to be sick anymore," she says she is proud of me for saying how I feel and gives me a hug.

My mom's therapist says it may take a long time for her to get well, but most people with MPD do feel better and can be regular moms again.

My mom's therapist calls her a "survivor." "Survivor" is a big word. It means that my mom was smart and strong and creative. She found a way to live through the bad things that happened to her. She did it by pretending in her mind that she wasn't really there when the bad things happened.

Sometimes, she pretended so hard that it felt like a different person was there. After all of this pretending, she started to really feel like there was more than one person inside her head.

Those different, inside "people" are still there, and sometimes they talk to her and to her therapist. My mom and her therapist call those inside people alters. One time one of them talked to me. My mom acted like a little girl and talked in a little girl's voice. She wanted to play with me. She acted silly, not like my mom at all. I didn't know what to do, so I played games with her and we had fun.

My mom says she has more than twenty-six alters in her head. She says that sometimes they fight with each other or yell at her. I don't hear anything, but my mom says it is going on in her head and I can't hear it. Some other people with MPD say they have more than 100 alters in their heads and we both can't imagine what that would be like.

Lots of times my mom has trouble believing that she has alters in her head. She would like them to just go away so she can be a regular mom again. But her therapist says she has to listen to them and find out what happened to them so the alters can learn to work together (and maybe someday go away).

The problem with MPD is that the alters my mom made up to protect herself still seem real to her now, even though the danger is over. They try to take over my mom and make her act like they want. That is when she acts strange and sometimes hurts herself or has to go to the hospital.

It is hard to have a mom with MPD. I get angry at her for having MPD. When she hurts herself or has to go to the hospital, I get afraid that she has gone away and will never come back. I wonder if she loves me. I feel like no one understands.

Most people don't know about MPD. Some people think my mom is just "acting." Other people say she must be crazy or they don't believe her. I believe her but I can't talk to my friends about it. They don't understand it. It's embarrassing to have a mom like mine. Mom and I talk about how hard it is for me sometimes and she tries to understand.

Sometimes we just hug and that helps.

On one of her bad days I wanted to cheer her up, so I asked if I could make her a cake. She said, "Yes." Soon she was in the kitchen trying to help me. We had a good time making a chocolate cake with lots of frosting. We love each other and I am proud of her because she is trying so hard to get better and she is proud of me, as well.

My mom says all families have problems and challenges, happy days and sad days. Ours are just different kinds of problems because my mom is different. Just like all other moms, mine is working hard to be the best mom she can be.

In our family we can talk about anything and we can tell each other how we feel. This makes us special. Even though we sometimes have troubles, I think we are a pretty good family because we love each other.

About the Author

Deborah Sessions, a multiple and loving mother, wrote this book for her children.

About the Sidran Foundation

The Sidran Foundation is a national non-profit organization devoted to advocacy, education, and research on behalf of people with severe psychiatric disabilities. A major focus of the foundation is the development of programs and projects for people with trauma generated psychological disorders and those who live and work with them.

In addition, the Sidran Foundation provides books, resources, and other information about dissociative disorders. For details write or phone, The Sidran Foundation, 2328 W. Joppa Road, Suite 15, Lutherville, MD 21093, (410) 825-8888.